Off to School!

adapted by Sascha Paladino
based on the screenplay written by Sascha Paladino
illustrated by Michael Scanlon, Little Airplane Productions

SIMON SPOTLIGHT/NICKELODEON
New York London Toronto Sydney

Based on the TV series *Wonder Pets!*™ as seen on Nickelodeon®

SIMON SPOTLIGHT
An imprint of Simon & Schuster Children's Publishing Division
1230 Avenue of the Americas, New York, New York 10020

Manufactured in the United States of America
10 9 8 7 6 5 4 3 2
ISBN: 978-1-4169-7197-9

Linny the Guinea Pig, Turtle Tuck, and Ming-Ming Duckling were sitting quietly in their cages. Suddenly the red tin-can phone started to ring!

The Wonder Pets rushed to answer the phone.

"Look," said Linny. "It's a baby blowfish!"

"She's at the bottom of the ocean!" said Ming-Ming.

"How can we help you?" asked Tuck as he looked into the phone.

The baby blowfish sang to the Wonder Pets:

Today's my first day of fish preschool.
Mama said it'll be cool.
But I don't know . . . I'm a little scared to go.

"That baby blowfish needs our help!" said Linny. "Let's go, Wonder Pets!"

Linny, Tuck, and Ming-Ming too!
We're Wonder Pets, and we'll help you!

The Wonder Pets worked together to build a special Flysub so they could go under the ocean!

"We are coming to help you, Baby Blowfish!" called Ming-Ming as the Flysub soared through the sky.

Wonder Pets, Wonder Pets, we're on our way!
To help a baby blowfish and save the day!
We're not too big and we're not too tough,
but when we work together we've got the right stuff!
Go, Wonder Pets! Yay!

The Wonder Pets landed at the bottom of the sea near the fish preschool. It looked like a nice place, but the baby blowfish was too scared to go inside!

"Hello, Baby Blowfish," said Linny, "You're going to love school! We'll go in with you to help you get used to it."

"That's a wonderful idea!" said Mama Blowfish.

The Wonder Pets and the blowfish swam into the preschool, where they met the teacher, Miss Sea Horse.

"Welcome to fish preschool!" said Miss Sea Horse. The baby blowfish looked around curiously.

"We have a big day today!" said Miss Sea Horse. "There's playtime and snack time and circle time. And after circle time, you go home!"

"Oh. That sounds great," said the baby blowfish. She was starting to feel a little bit better.

“Is that a sandbox?” she asked, pointing to the school’s sandbox.

“Come on,” said Ming-Ming. “Let’s go play!”

Ming-Ming and the baby blowfish built a castle in the sand.

A baby squid swam by. "Ooh," said the baby squid. "Nice sand castle!"

Ming-Ming whispered to the baby blowfish, "Why don't you ask the baby squid to play with us?"

"Um," said the baby blowfish shyly, "would you like to play?"

"Yes!" said the baby squid. And just like that, the baby blowfish made a new friend!

Then it was time for Mama Blowfish to leave. "Have fun today," she said.

Oh, no! The baby blowfish didn't want her mama to leave! "I don't want to be at school if you're not going to be here!" she said.

"Your mama has to leave," said Tuck. "Preschool isn't for mommies, right?"

"That's right," said Linny. "But mommies always come back."

But the baby blowfish was really upset. She didn't want her mama to go!

"This is serious!" said Ming-Ming.

“I know,” said Linny. “We can sing Baby Blowfish a song to let her know that her mama will always come back!”

The Wonder Pets sang:

**Wherever you are, whatever you do,
she’ll always, always come back for you!**

The song made the baby blowfish feel much better.

"I'll be back after circle time," promised Mama Blowfish. "Have fun with your new friends!" She kissed her baby and swam away.

ABC
123

The baby blowfish looked around and saw some blocks. She swam up to a baby starfish and a baby crab and asked, “Can I play?”

“Sure!” they said.

The new friends built a big block tower that reached high in the sky!

Then Miss Sea Horse called, "Circle time!"

Baby Blowfish danced with all her new friends!

"I think the baby blowfish really likes preschool," said Linny.

And before long Mama Blowfish came back! Just like she said she would! The baby blowfish was so happy to see her. "I had the best day!" said the baby blowfish. "Thanks for your help, Wonder Pets!"

"You're welcome!" said the Wonder Pets. "This calls for some celery!"

And they all shared celery with raisins on it.